ISBN 978-0-86037-333-9

MUSLIM CHILDREN'S LIBRARY

ALLAH THE MAKER SERIES

Allah Gave Me A Nose To Smell

Author: *Rizwana Qamaruddin*
Illustrator & Designer: *Stevan Stratford*
Co-ordinator: *Raana Bokhari*

Published by
The Islamic Foundation
Markfield Conference Centre
Ratby Lane, Markfield
Leicester LE67 9SY
United Kingdom
E publications@islamic-foundation.com
W www.islamic-foundation.com

Quran House, PO Box 30611, Nairobi, Kenya

PMB 3193, Kano, Nigeria

Distributed by
Kube Publishing Ltd.
T +44(0)1530 249230
F +44(0)1530 249656
E info@kubepublishing.com

Printed in China by Midas Printing International Limited

British Library Cataloguing in Publication Data

Qamaruddin, Rizwana
Allah Gave me a nose to smell. - (Allah the maker series)
1. Smell - Juvenile literature 2. Smell - Religious aspects -
Islam - Juvenile literature 3. Nose - Juvenile literature
4. Nose - Religious aspects - Islam - Juvenile literature
I. Title II. Islamic Foundation
612.8'6
ISBN 0860373339

Allah Gave Me

A NOSE
TO SMELL

Rizwana Qamaruddin

Illustrated by Stevan Stratford

THE ISLAMIC FOUNDATION

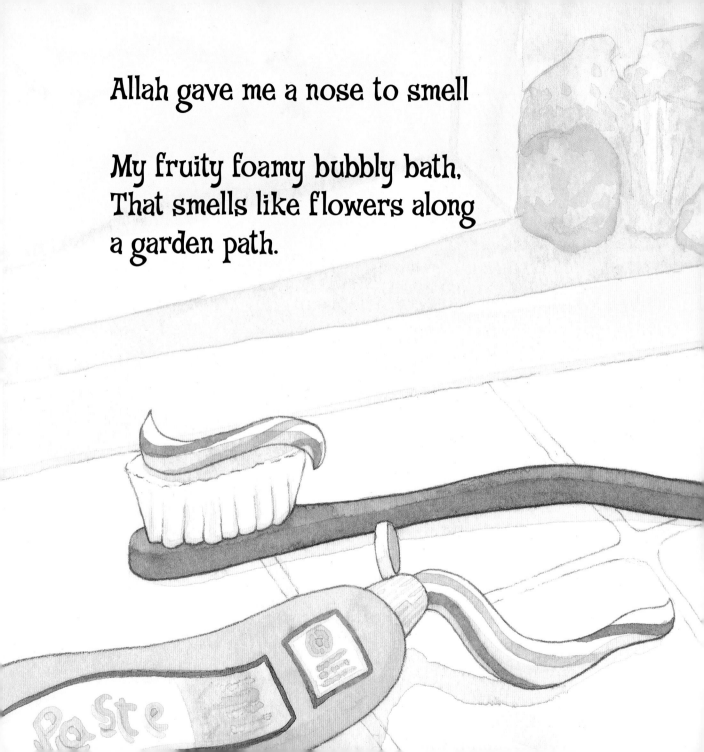

Allah gave me a nose to smell

My fruity foamy bubbly bath,
That smells like flowers along
a garden path.

My squidgey, squelchy mint toothpaste
Which my tongue can also taste.

My talcum powder so chalky and white.
I've put on too much - oh what a sight!

The fragrance of itar in the air
When Daddy goes for the Jum'ah prayer.

Allah gave me a nose to wiggle
When I see a baby wriggle.

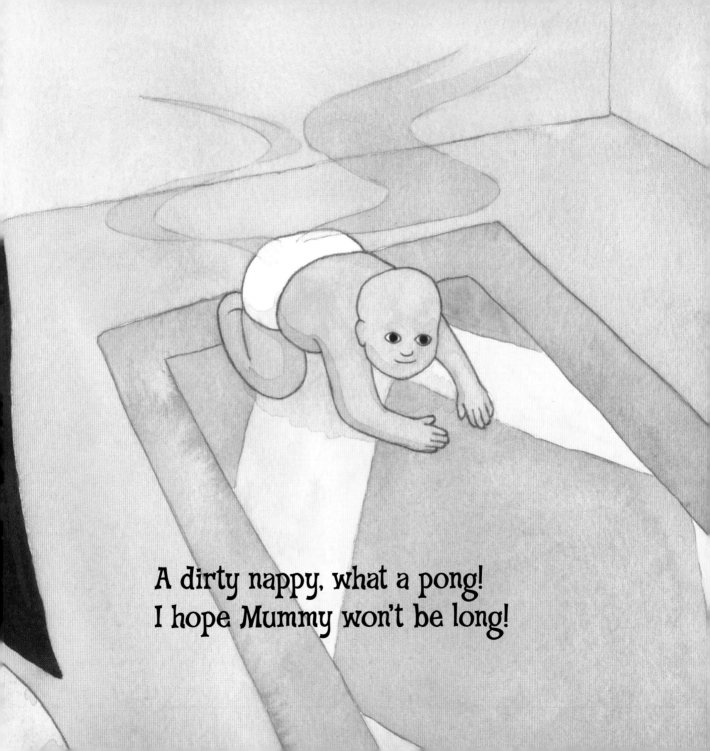

A dirty nappy, what a pong!
I hope Mummy won't be long!

Allah gave me a nose to smell
What's for dinner – I can tell!

It's my favourite fish and chips
I think it's time to lick my lips!

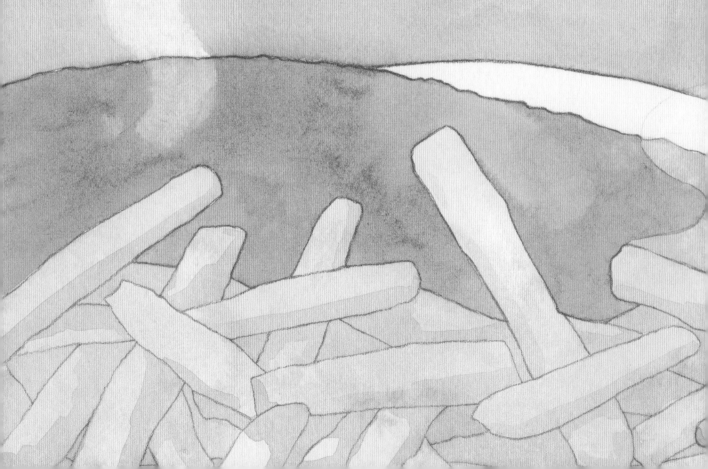

Iftar is here – lets take our seat.
I smell the foods I love to eat.

Before we start say bismillah.
Then we recite the sawm du'a.

Allah gave me a nose to smell!

The sweet scent of a bright red rose!
The freshness of my new washed clothes.

The barbecue at Eid just brings
Smells of many delicious things!

Burgers, kebabs and corn on the cob.
To cook it all is Daddy's job!

And what will my favourite
milk shake be

Banana, vanilla, or strawberry?

Allah gave me a nose
to warn me,
Of the dangers that
might harm me.

Like a smoking, burning pan,
And a fire as it began.

Pepper always makes me sneeze.
Smoke makes me cough and wheeze.

And as I open a dirty bin
That my teddy's fallen in,

'Keep away' my Mummy tells me.
I can smell it's really dirty!

But when I have a cold that is bad,
Nothing smells good – I'm very sad!

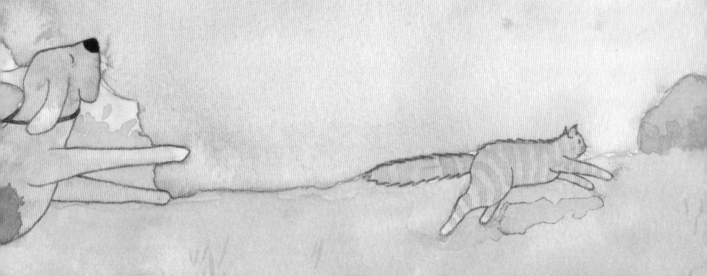

Allah gave me a nose to smell
And to other creatures as well!

Thank you Allah for my nose,
And for my mouth,
eyes, ears,
fingers and toes!

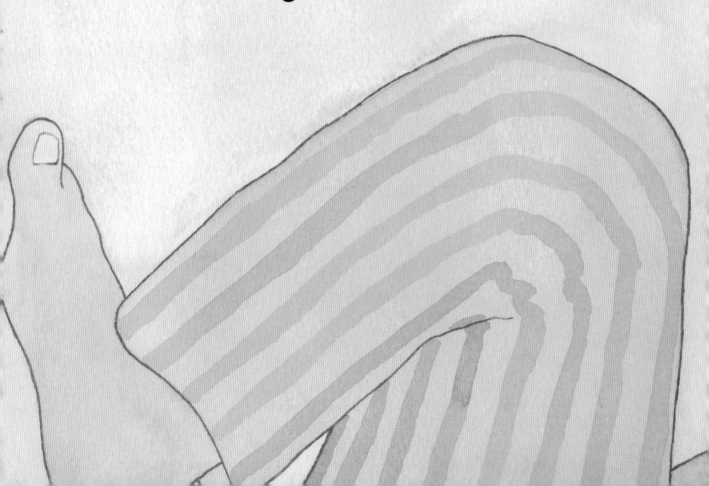